If I Found a Wistful Unicorn

To Martin

Published by
PEACHTREE PUBLISHERS
1700 Chattahoochee Avenue
Atlanta, Georgia 30318-2112

www.peachtree-online.com

Text © 1978 by Ann Ashford
Illustrations © 1978 by Wilfred H. Drath

Printed and bound in Singapore
Illustrations painted in watercolor on cold press illustration board

10 9 8 7 6 5 4 3 2 1
Anniversary Edition

ISBN 1-56145-271-8

Cataloging-in-Publication Data is available from the Library of Congress.

If I Found a Wistful Unicorn

A Gift of Love

Anniversary Edition

Ann Ashford
Illustrated by Bill Drath

PEACHTREE
ATLANTA

If I found a wistful unicorn and
brought him to you, all forlorn...
Would you pet him?

If I took an empty midnight train

across the country in the rain...

Would you meet me?

If I picked a little flower up
and put it in a paper cup…

Would you smell it?

If I found a secret place to go,

with you the only one to know...

Would you be there?

If my cricket coughed and got the flu

and needed warmth and comfort too…
          Would you hold him?

If my rainbow were to turn all gray
and wouldn't shine at all today…

Would you paint it?

If my birch tree were afraid at night
and couldn't sleep without a light…

Would you bring one?

If my soul were feeling all alone
and wasn't near a telephone…

Would you write to it?

If my clock developed nervous strain

TICK   TICK   TICK

and needed help to "tock" again...

Would you fix it?

If I ran backwards up a tree

and called for you to follow me…

Would you do it?

If my turtle got a nervous tic and
couldn't swim 'cause he was sick…

Would you sit with him?

If I said that I could dance for you
as hard as that would be to do…

Would you watch me?

If my pet turnip turned on me

and bit me fiercely on the knee…

Would you bandage it?

If my obelisk came tumbling down
and fell in pieces on the ground...

Would you pick it up?

If my nightingale were a monotone

and much too shy to sing alone...

Would you hum with him?

If my wart decided yesterday

to be a dimple anyway…

Would you notice?

If all that I would want to do

would be to sit and talk to you…

Would you listen?

If any of these things you'll do,

I'll never have to say to you...

"Do you love me?"

ABOUT THE AUTHOR
Ann Ashford
1939–1988

Ann Ashford was born in Hannibal, Missouri, and raised on the Upper Peninsula of Michigan. She graduated from Agnes Scott College in 1961 and was a United Methodist church worker for migrants, a welfare caseworker, a teacher, an actress, and the vice-president of a family-owned fund-raising consulting firm.

IF I FOUND A WISTFUL UNICORN was the first book published by Peachtree Publishers. It won the Award for Juvenile Literature from the Council of Authors and Journalists.

ABOUT THE ILLUSTRATOR
Bill Drath
1915–1991

Bill Drath was born in Wisconsin. A graduate of the University of Wisconsin, he served in the army during World War II and the Korean War, retiring in 1966 as a lieutenant colonel. In addition to IF I FOUND A WISTFUL UNICORN, Drath also illustrated WILLOWCAT AND THE CHIMNEY SWEEP, SOUTHERN IS…, and WHEN SOMEONE DIES.

ABOUT THE PUBLISHER
Helen Elliott
1921–1983

Helen Elliott founded Peachtree Publishers in May 1977. Having survived a bout with cancer, she decided to act on her lifelong dream of establishing a publishing house in the South. She met artist Bill Drath, another cancer survivor, who showed her a poem by a friend of his. Ann Ashford's inspiring words, illustrated by Drath, became the first book published by the new company, and Helen Elliott's dream was born.